Just Being

A journey from being born a daughter to being home to mother

Just Being

A journey from being born a daughter to being home to mother

Dr. Sujatha Arun (M.D)

ZORBA BOOKS

Published by Zorba Books, March 2022

Website: www.zorbabooks.com
Email: info@zorbabooks.com

Author Name & Copyright © **Dr. Sujatha Arun (M.D)**
Email of the author :- **drsujathaarun@gmail.com**
Title :- **Just Being**

Printbook ISBN :-978-93-93029-86-7
Ebook ISBN :-978-93-93029-87-4

The publisher under the guidance and direction of the author has published the contents in this book, and the publisher takes no responsibility for the contents, its accuracy, completeness, any inconsistencies, or the statements made. The contents of the book do not reflect the opinion of the publisher or the editor. The publisher and editor shall not be liable for any errors, omissions, or the reliability of the contents of the book.

Any perceived slight against any person/s, place or organization is purely unintentional.

Zorba Books Pvt. Ltd. (opc)
Sushant Arcade,
Next to Courtyard Marriot,
Sushant Lok 1, Gurgaon – 122009, India

*Dedicated to my Mother for I consider myself
so blessed to be born her daughter.*

Love you, Mom.

*In deep reverence and gratitude to my Father,
for teaching me to look at Life with curiosity.
He taught me patience and hard work
and always bought me the
new book instead of the new dress.*

Contents

Preface

This book is a true story. To readers who may read it with utter disbelief, I say, in all humility, to please treat it as fiction, for now I know that every work of fiction, is a true story in itself, because it has already happened in the mind of that extremely blessed story teller. Between those imaginative thoughts and the experience, is the writing or better still, the filming. When we understand our own story, we are gifted with the ability to understand those of other authors, and with shared ground, understanding becomes easier, conflicts less.

When one understands their own story, they will wait to hear those of the other- this is a natural progression of curiosity in nature- and suddenly everyone is understanding every one else- and there is a common dream of no climate change, no terrorism, no poverty and most important of all- no narcissicism. Out goes judgement and selfishness and in comes curiosity, humility, love and compassion.

And to think that I was born in a country which always had these teachings in its core – India- in two terms which used be a common, sure boring recital in our Sanskrit classrooms in school-

Vasudhaiva Kutumbakam

Paropakaramartha Idam Shariram

What a privilege to be born to my Mom and in this country!!!!!

Surely if there's heaven, this is that.

Sometimes people call me a voodoo doctor- that's ok, voodoo doctors don't share their trade secrets- but here I'm baring it all!!

Sometimes doctors call me psychic- that's ok too- the psychic are waiting to be heard too☺

Sometimes doctors say I'm "Bhatki hui"(Hindi- gone astray from my regular stream), that's ok but really I've never understood medicine better, in all these years of practice put together. But one thing they all agree is that I am a good doctor. Feels nice to know that but I'm a better doctor only now.

ONE

When you are helplessly part of the system
(you don't even know you don't want to be part of)

Staying Present With Guilt

My Mom and Dad had probably a slightly better than a neonate marriage. Mother was 13 and father was 21 with a difference of nine years. I was born to my mother when she was 15 and people generally thought we were sisters. Mom came from a very forward-looking family, and Dad from a heavily orthodox family. Although introverted, in their core was a simplicity, a great gift I am repository of, from my Dad's lineage- the capacity of hard work.

(They won't take it easy, even if it came easy.:)

My mother was the opposite end of that spectrum.

She lived by social interactions, smiles, intelligence and laughter and games of chess between her Grandmom and Dad that were generally won by her Grandmom and heated arguments after that.

It must have been so difficult to restrain herself in the orthodoxy of my Dad's family.

Well, she did that, curtailing all that she was capable of. She bore three children before she was 22.

Soon we had to leave Chennai and move to Bangalore. We found a better than a chawl type of accommodation. Those years would turn out to be the best for us children.

I was put in a school and was a privilege to have gone to the school.

Away from all the environmental control of Chennai, my Mom allowed herself to flower.

My Dad was extremely hard-working. An engineer with "The Hindu" newspaper. For more than 20 years he worked only night shift with little sleep in the day time. This permanently altered his neuronal pathways, and he was to suffer Parkinson's disease as a occupational hazard.

Together they raised us three children giving all they had, sweat and blood, not asking for anything in return. I went to medical school and although it was govt seat in a private college the fees was heavy for those times.

My Dad would take advance from his Diwali bonus and pay it off.

They never borrowed. They never aspired for much.

My Mom had a great quality I didn't know I was repository of, too. She would be happy, very happy in the presence of the moment it did not take much at all.

The mismatch between Mom and Dad soon became evident but the damage was done. There were moments of severe conflict at home and as children we fought hard to not take sides but that was difficult as my Dad found me to confide in and my Mom probably my brother.

When expected to hold that space, it is very hard for a 10 or 13-year-olds to not judge and I did just that.

Took the cause of my Dad but even at that age I felt deeply for my Mom. I loved her to the depth of my bones but couldn't help myself when I picked up fights with her.

She died due to triple negative breast cancer - a cancer that has a will like no other, a mind of its own and absolutely destructive in its course.

Her death was a horror movie to say the least, a suffering that was unrelenting until she gave up dying fighting. As her children we were numbed to the bones and I don't think one can come out of that without being transformed. For if not moved by that sacrifice, life isn't worth it.

My mother died for us.

Now the good part-the guilt I felt was the chink through which she entered me during my transformation and now firmly residing inside of me, guiding me through every activity sometimes to the point of annoyance.

Hey come on, that's doesn't seem practical right? That someone can live inside of you? Read on………

Love you, Mom

1.1

The BAT Analogy

Ever wondered how Bats host corona viruses inside of them without ever being affected by them? Ever heard of any Bat that died of Covid19?

I have always wondered what makes Bats so non chalant about them being host to that tiny speck of a virus that is taking the human species by a storm of such mammoth proportions.

Bats are at the lowest level of mammalian differentiation. That's about how, we humans are similar to Bats. We are both mammals.

Bats are day blind(I haven't checked this fact☺, its out of reading), but have a razor sharp night vision and are nocturnal animals. They live in forests and caves and in spooky places. They cannot manufacture their own food, so they have to fly out of their comfort zones(imagine a day blind pilot flying a plane you are in☺), how do they find their way back home?

For this movement- to enable search for food, Bats have two tremendous natural adaptations for survival. Echolocation- being able to sense UHF (Ultra High Frequency) sound waves and magnetolocation- sense the polar North. Secure in these adaptations, Bats can throw caution to the winds (pun intended☺), they fly high and far and still find their way back home, and day blindness is not even a bother!!!

But what about corona viruses?

This is an acquired adaptation for Bats. Its an example of seamlessness of existence in nature. Corona viruses, composed of a mere group of nucleotides are nothing but dust particles outside of an animal cell. They need animal cells to host them. The Bat complies this request with elan and in return finds itself totally repugnant to the most advanced mammalian species – Homo sapiens sapiens. How smart is that, you would say. I say so and how exciting this symbiosis in nature, how beautifully self-sustaining.

Bats simply love their corona viruses because they confer survival advantage to them. It's a win-win situation, right there, not a word spoken, just acceptance of nature offered protection by both species.

Suddenly some mishap happens and the virus finds itself in a strange new host- the humans. Everything seems so different- it does not seem to understand the ways of the humans. They seem to have the licence to kill and keep on pulling out arms after arms that go by the name of antibody and cell mediated stuff. The virus that is now totally confused, jumps from one host to another, in a desperate attempt to find the good old Bat friend.

Not being able to go back to its original host, the virus has to learn to adapt- and what better adaptation, than to escape detection, to lie low? Nature has simple mechanisms for simple souls-and for the corona virus, it just has to knock off a couple or two of its nucleotides.....

Once silent, everything seems ok for a while. Phew! Some rest now.....

As the virus rests, humans are back to doing what they want to do-keep themselves busy in pursuit of their external goals, and they are not paying attention to their own body.....

Suddenly, after a lull, the virus finds itself an innocent bystander to various other diseases of the human, such as diabetes, cancer and also the treatment of these conditions., the virus may soon find itself homeless if it doesn't send an SOS....

The human is not able to produce antibodies like before, so the virus surfaces now, multiplying, in a final bid to protect itself....

Can we help the virus find the Bat?

Are you kidding, you may ask.

I am not. If we can host the corona viruses like the BAT?

Is that even possible?

I think that is. If we can become Bats ourselves.

How and how would know you when you transform to Batman or Batwoman?

And here it is pertinent to note that children are less prone to Covid- 19.

Read on......

Two

What A Blessing Of Teenhood!!

The time of life my Mom did not get to enjoy.

The first 15 years of life do matter and the school matters a lot.

When our school friends last a life time, life is always young.

For all his heavy orthodoxy at home, my paternal Grandpa (the one who extend his patriarchal authority over my Mom, but who was also gentle with her), he put us three children in a British school, in Chennai.

We would see him reciting the Ramayan at home everyday. But he never imposed any religious rituals on us and would help us find tender palm leaves, to help us celebrate Sabbath Day, in school.

We were taught scripture in school. Our day would start with dear Mrs. Felix, our Principal, presiding over hymn recital. We had a cute little hymn book we carried to school everyday.

I would score the maximum in school scripture exams and once, when I had malaria in the midst of a math exam,, my scripture marks were transferred to my math column- by my dear class teacher, Mrs. King. Life was so simple. Mrs. King had probably felt that if I could do well in scripture, what the heck, I could do well in math too!!

When we shifted to Bangalore, I ended up in a completely Hindu school and though there was a sea of difference, the essence of teaching and the kindness of the teachers were the same. So blessed we were to have been taught by their league. I took to the school immediately, and there were lots of teachings from Bhagavadgita, imparted to us by the founding Guru Swamiji, himself.

From a girl's school, I had gone to co-ed school. There were lots of opportunities for teenage exuberance. I made friends thick and fast. We still are a huge group, after a gap of 39 years.

The girls were a special lot and I was to know later, that many of them would be mediators, in the course of my transformation.

I was aware that gender is just an identity (like a name) and so was religion. And that at the heart of living was our own identity, regardless of gender or religion. The first step toward losing our identity is to recognize that we have a separate identity of our own. And teenhood helps us know our identity- in terms of gender, religion, and our core feelings.

My Mom had not had a chance to develop her own identity.

In this school too, there was no enforcement and teachers would just have a moment with you, with gentle concern of our errant activities.

Somehow marks seemed secondary and I vividly remember of wanting to be present in school every day and that school was fun!

Three

There Is An Indian Term, "Vaidyonarayano Harihi". To Me, This Term Says That The Doctor Is God Himself, In Physical Form. That's How I Feel Toward The Neurologist Who Diagnosed My Mom's Epilepsy Of Late Onset As Temporal Lobe Epilepsy (TLE), Put Her On Carbamazepine, And Virtually Cured Her Of It, For It Never Came Back Even When She Was Struggling To Breathe During The Last Days Of Her Mere 61 Year Life.

My Grandad could never make it to Bangalore. After his death, my Dad's step sister (attai in Tamil) came to stay with us. She was totally adorable and now I realise, pure consciousness in existence.

The next ten years were the most karmically intensive period for our family including my attai. My parents worked hard, funding our education and giving us 2 square meals of absolutely delectable food at home. The coffee was fresh and heavenly. We were secure in their presence. My mother never ever asked for anything for herself. She just wanted to *be* herself. My father spent the time that he was not asleep, in praying and performing the daily "aradhanai" (Tamil- Worship)

The devotion to their common purpose of raising us three children was unparalled and I don't think even I can manage that for my own children.

Gratitude overwhelms me when I think of their sacrifice.

The strife was much more than what is expressed here, the type that cannot be remembered without crying.

We lost our attai, when I was doing my undergraduation. She was admitted for fracture tibia- I could visit her every day and give her nursing care- the nurses willingly taught me a lot about nursing including how to make the hospital bed. She finally died of bronchopneumonia. She was the first elder I had personally cared for and I had enjoyed the process, sad after her demise.

As I was finishing my internship, my Mom had the first symptom of having led the restrained life of no autonomy- Epilepsy. We were quite shocked when it happened the first time and then again and again.

My Dad put my youngest brother in the hostel(he was in the final year of undergraduate engineering) and shifted base to Chennai. I was doing my postgraduation in Mangalore.

She was diagnosed to have TLE and put on Carbamazepine. The frequency came down and even though painfully and slowly, she was able to regulate the dosage herself and finally was able to stop it completely.

When the diagnosis is correct and the medicine perfect, the result is nothing short of magic.

And could life itself be the quest for the correct diagnosis of our purpose? If yes, life itself can become rich and beautiful..........

Four

If We Do Not Have A Heart Break, We Can Never Appreciate True Love In All Its Entirety.

A puppy love gone sour, Ravi Shastry had found someone interesting and a heart break with a person who wanted me to move to America, on my own merit, if I wanted to marry him.

Even as child of probably 8 or 10, I didn't want to go the favorite destination of most Iyengar lads- the USA. Every marriage had mamis (tamil- middle aged women, addressed with respect) discussing where their children lived in the US and whether it was possible to to get them married off so their children don't have to deal with the uncertainties of Indian partners like me, with a quirky resolution to stay back and be present, for their parents. If you weren't in the US you didn't make the cut.

My parents wanted me to get married, understandably so. There was a beeline of prospective grooms, with lucrative jobs in the US. After a couple of them, they all seemed the same and boring.

Then magic happened. My lovely neighbour suggested her nephew and things moved fast that he could come to meet me. There was something very genuine about him. And his attitude was one to embrace when he said that he would care for my parents like he cared for his own.!!!!

What then could stop me from saying YES! YES! YES! I had found my man.

A and I were married in Bangalore. It was a simple, no fanfare wedding, with the convergence of all good things.

I went back to Mangalore, to complete my MD in Pathology.

Everyone believed that I had been an extremely capable student but fell short of optimum performance for the level of expectations. I was used to this for I had been like this from school and considered marks a small part of the entire experience. This trait helped to not judge my children by marks and the comfort of nonjudgement turned them into the most humane and loving children one can be parent to. A feather I love to wear on my cap.

My man, A, is the most remarkable human being I have encountered in my life. He is severely non-conformist (many times more than I).

He has the tremendous ability to be present in the moment and an extreme ability to get things done.

When I came to Mumbai after competing my post-graduation, I found A to be the son every parent would wish for. Every pie that he earned (or I earned) was to be shared with his Mother, Father and his Grandmother. (His uncle lived in the US and A was more than willing to take care of her, here in India). His father could only travel business class, his mother could only be chauffeur driven even to the grocery store that was 500 m from home. His mother got the better saree and the bigger chunk of jewellery. His generosity did not stop there. In its ambit fell his sister, my sis-in law and my nieces and my parents. I had never witnessed this kind of selflessness before and happy that he could buy and look after his parents the way he did. It made me so happy.

My pockets were always full, never ever was I told to moderate my spending.

Suddenly, one day in 2009, his business project had a setback because investors moved out. But my laboratory service was at its zenith, my lab had become a household name in my community.

Money was coming in and enough to support a reasonably standard lifestyle although maybe not like before.

The next decade was to be the next karmically intensive period, for me, now with A.

Five

Never Let An Opportunity To Show Love For Your Mother Go By, She Is The Centre Of The Universe.

A's Grandmother, who was finding it difficult to carry on at age 95, was brought to stay with us. There was not a single worrisome ailment in her, except that she was prone to falls. She was simple and adorable and my children and I got along famously with her.

In April of 2011, my Mom and Dad came to visit us as they were leaving for a period of 6 months to the US, where my brothers live.

My Mom complained of a small nodule in her left breast and it was painful for her to raise the arm. That was the beginning of her journey into cancer and end of that journey to America.

She was diagnosed to have TNBC (Triple Negative Breast Cancer) and the next 11/4 years of her life would teach me how restriction of autonomy, at every turn of life can have a devastating effect on the body, because the body keeps the score of every uL of saliva that is swallowed for not being able to express itself.

That 11/4 years that began in April 2011 and ended on July 19, 2012, would have a complete purging effect on my system, to its very core, a suffering that can never be described in words, a suffering that can squeeze one out of all ego, assumptions and falsehoods. The emotional trauma of Mom's sufferings and my helplessness could have become extremely telling on me- had it not been for the three men in my life- A and my two children.

Thank you, dear ones, I feel extreme gratitude and extreme love.

The caregivers must be the focus. They not only handle the emotional trauma of the most loved ones' sufferings, but they have to battle the environmental systems and societal recommendations and beliefs.

Some society - tuned individuals believed that it was the Sons' duty to care for parents, not Daughters'. That this patriarchal belief can never be challenged. I found that let alone the treatment of cancer, even the environment of care can throw up challenges at the most important moment, and I was never fully equipped to handle them, these ruthless belief systems, never held for questioning ever before.

My Dad had his first knee replacement operation, after having been diagnosed to have Parkinson's disease and was on Dopa.

A's Grandmother had a fall in an unsupervised moment and had a hip fracture.

In April 2012, I was looking after Mom who was having terminal cancer, totally bedridden with a massive pleural effusion and A's grandmother who had inoperable hip fracture.

When things go wrong, the right has to come up, as existence has continuity. The right s were my doctor friends, S and S- Gratitude to them I feel is immense. As I was being swept by this "Chakravyuha", these lovely friends of mine were conspiring- and I got a call from Dr. S, that I was to shift the Grandmother to her nursing home where she would be given nursing care and I can look after Mom. Dr. S(the other S) and A, physically handled the transfer of Grandmother, as I was away at the hospital as Mom was in the ICU.

A month later, Grandmother had me called. She took my hand, stroked it gently and spoke the following sentence in Tamil.

"There's only one person I feel bad to leave and go, and that is you". She kissed my hand and an hour later slipped into coma and died a few hours later.

I cry every time I think of this act of generosity and my heart swells with gratitude to be blessed by a great soul. The day April 27, 2012.

Approximately 2 months later, I was holding my Mom's hand, as she put in great effort to breathe her last. I was numb, sitting by her side, totally helpless. I felt I had failed as a doctor no doubt, but I had failed as a daughter too for I had not asked for forgiveness I had wanted from her- for all the harsh words spoken and for all the moments of my judgement of her. I felt naked, totally exposed and an utter failure

To the world I had been an ideal daughter, having done all for the mother, but to myself, I wasn't all the good daughter that the world was making me out to be.

The guilt I housed – was the chink that would ultimately open the doors of light wide open for me. But at that time, I was unaware.

Post her death, immediately and for approximately 4 years, I felt as if I had 2/3rd of my life with Mom. My Dad wouldn't allow me to cry as he said he wouldn't be able to handle it. My bereavement was extending year after year and I just wanted to be done with Arun, children, Dad and my in-in-laws and join my Mom, just to hold her tight and say sorry.

Unaware to me, a process of mind- body coordination has set in. My poor body, my heart included, wanted to live, it felt young, it wanted to take the lessons of Moms death and help others. But the guilt in my mind was a difficult tenant. It was making my body go the other way- and I was producing antibodies against the first class of non-me relationship- food. I was getting slowly intolerant to even common foodstuff. But I was aware that I loved and enjoyed food, every type of it, vegetable shopping was my best stress buster and colors of fruits and vegetables was a cheap way to get high!

If help had not arrived, I would soon be producing auto antibodies- antibodies against one's own cells, including those of neurons. I could have had rapid onset dementia and a traffic free highway to reach my Mom.

Only, Mom was not going to have any of that and she was planning her own.

Love you Mom, hugs and kisses.

And I get this strange feeling that A's Grandmom is a co conspirator☺

Six

A, my soul mate, watched me quietly. He was waiting for my attention, the hand holding, the sweet pecks on the cheek and the tight hugs. They had all disappeared, just like that.

He put it all aside, these carnal requirements and helped me again, to relocate my Dad from Chennai to Mumbai. We bought a moderately spacious apartment for him close by.

Dad shifted and the first thing I did was to get the other knee replaced. As I sat alone in the hospital, in the waiting room, I thought of Mom, having looked after him, for the first knee replacement, a mere 5 months before her death. How difficult it must've been, to have gone up and down the lifts, helping him with the pot and so on…. And she had never spoken word.

In Dec 2017, my Dad suddenly developed a wrist drop. I brought him to stay with us at our home and then he had shifted permanently.

My Dad lived with me, through his worsening Parkinson's, severe dementia, troublesome morbid constipation, falls, paranoid attacks, one of which took his life. My Dad passed away in Oct 2019, 2 years after moving to my place and just 4 months before lockdown. Caring for him during the Pandemic would have been an extremely difficult thing for us.

A week before his death, he had smilingly told me that he would be gone in a week. I remember I had said a prayer for his peaceful passing for there was no strength in me to go through another difficult death of a parent. 6 days later, my Dad had a strange request for coffee just before dinner. He didn't want dinner.

The next morning, wasn't unusual at all. He had bathed and had coffee. As I was passing his room, I saw him to have a fixed stare, quiet tears rolling down his cheeks. I called out to him but he was not listening and as I helped him to the cot, he breathed his last. He was gone, just like that.

Nothing can prepare one for a parent's death. There was one difference though, this time around. I was free to cry and cry I did, at every opportunity, and sure enough, today, the death or absence does not evoke the same degree of regret as my Mom's did.

As for A, he was still waiting, in love, and between us almost a decade had gone by......

At this point, I felt that someone out there knew what was going to happen ahead of time. For the first time I had a glimpse of divine timing as well as timelessness. I made a note of that.

Seven

*Help Does Arrive, When The Unanswered Questions Are
Literally And Figuratively, Burning You Up*

2 years before the pandemic, there was awareness that the field of Pathology was changing- It was becoming more and more process oriented, moving away from patient contact (which can make it unbearably boring) and there were price wars of unimaginable scale. This was a field I could not bring myself to play in. But the users of my service, namely the beautiful people of Chembur(a suburb in Mumbai) with whom I could connect individually and as a community, would need my services for some more time. So I prayed for someone to pick it up, run it in about the same way that I had run mine- i.e. have a culture fit. I did find a buyer. The acquisition went smoothly, totally done by A, and although I have done my MBA too, I hadn't actually experienced "corporate" culture.

All was going well except that A kept reminding me, much to my chagrin, that I must remember I was now working for a corporate set up, and here, giving more than what is asked for is not appropriate. There was no need to go out of the way. The logic, I could never understand. Then the Pandemic struck.

During this time, I rediscovered myself as a Pathologist, and put all that I knew to innovate and set up collection of nasopharyngeal swabs for RTPCR testing. The innovations born out of necessity to offer collection services to the people of Chembur, had hundreds of patients coming in. The safe collection methods ensured that none among the lab staff had any covid infection, including I, and there was very little staff absenteeism. Soon services picked up with a robustness I have never seen before. My heart was singing but somewhere in the corner of heart I missed the reckoning that was due to me by the concerned bosses.

I left the service in March, 2021. And wasn't persuaded to stay back☺.

For the first time in my life, I was spending time with myself. We have a beautiful, well-ventilated house in an upmarket area of Chembur. It has a balcony that overlooks a dense canopy of trees. It is bathed by sunlight through the huge French windows adorning every room, including the kitchen.

I was just being myself, cooking for my family. My body was relaxed and my reflux disorder (GERD) was reducing.

I was reading books making Amazon happy by spending a substantial amount on the books I buy from their shelf.

These are the wonderful books I ordered and read, generally in a day. Once there's a book in hand, I suffer OCD of wanting to finish it in a day!!! I just can't help myself.

Zen Yoga by P.J. Saher.

I had started the first of the three steps toward self-integration, but I wasn't doing it so regularly.

There was a sense of Gratitude filling up inside me. My feet felt firm on the ground, and I felt calm, away from all the chaos outside.

Suddenly I felt an urge to get creative- and I was toying with the idea of having a "breath clinic" may be, if only to create awareness of importance of proper breathing. Outside there were deaths due to lack of Oxygen and the second wave was wreaking havoc.

Another book I finished in a day – **Early Indians by Tony Joseph.**

The research by the author was so comprehensive, I was amazed by the depth and more so because I am a pathologist and I understand sequencing techniques and The Human Genome Project.

And just like that, I ordered and read the book- **Accessing the Healing Power of Vagus – by Dr. Rosenberg.**

I could in a very subtle way connect things said in Tony Joseph's book and the book by Dr. Rosenberg and somehow there was a feeling that many pieces of a puzzle were connecting.

My school friend, another S ☺, suggested that I do a Wellness course and that she is finding it extremely rewarding to do it.

She also forwarded a 2-hour film- **Thrive**- in which a 64 point geometric figure has been analyzed and how there are evidences (like increased EMR) to prove that we do have visitors from other places in the Universe, that they have found a technology that does not use fossil fuel. The movie held me to trance, and I watched it in one go.

The wellness course was on. Our instructress, J, was simply amazing. I couldn't have imagined that we have technology that can connect to another part of the world, miles away. This person was going to change my life forever. How can it even by conjectured?

I couldn't help but remember P.J.Saher's words- That when the critical stage is reached, The guru(s) will appear.

Eight

The Guru Appears

In one of the classes, as part of being coachee, I mentioned that I sometimes had palpitations (extrasystoles) and didn't want to have it. J intervened, to introduce me to a simple somatic- of holding my heart. She asked me to just be with it for a brief while. It felt good and my heart felt quiet.

The class ended at half past 10 in the night. I went to bed, lying on my left and holding my heart with my right palm, almost cradling it. For the first time in almost a decade, I slept sound, it was the best sleep ever. In the morning, it felt beautifully refreshing and calm with a clarity of mind that was amazing. Life felt beautiful and seemed to hold a lot of promise.

Can one feel like that just by holding the heart? I felt a deep sense of gratitude to J and to my heart! How much my heart had supported me, through the roller coaster of my life, setting up palpitations and then gathering itself up, to become normal again. My heart had been witness to every moment of my life, including the formation of my brain, for during embryogenesis, heart is the first to show as sign of life. Any mother would testify to this as she would know the joy of her baby's heartbeat, at merely 15 days of conception!

I felt I was now speaking to my heart, like a mother to child, and it felt beautiful, and heart seemed to understand my language!

I became aware I have always been a person of heart- this sublime quality- an ultimate gift of my parents. Both were people of heart.

As part of the wellness course, I was volunteer coaching my doctor friend's mother, who had repeated sweating episodes for the last 30 years or so. The onset had been after her breast surgery. My doctor friend told me that she felt this was post-surgery and she felt some nerve had been affected by surgery.

I noted a coincidence for just that morning I had read from Dr. Rosenberg's book that surgical scars do influence the nervous system. But I was not making an important connection- that was to be the final piece of the puzzle….

To us doctors, a well healed scar is surgeon's pride. Whatever the procedure inside, a well healed scar is a reminder to both patient and doctor, of a job well done. The patient would generally feel thankful to the surgeon and wear the scar as small war wound- as it would represent trauma that was overcome.

As an intern, I had diligently dressed a patient of transvesical prostatectomy (an old way of prostate gland removal by incising the urinary bladder. Now this a minimally damaging surgery, with access through the urethra, TURP) to complete healing and in return, received a huge bag of fresh vegetables from his farm.

As a pathologist, I was approached by a friend to dress a wound of C-section (Caesarean section) that was not healing for six months. I tried my hand, mustering all the knowledge I could, and the scar healed in two weeks, and I became the recipient of a huge bottle of delectable garlic pickle.

8.1

❀

Night Of Happening (NOH)

That night in May 2021, after I had burped out all the gas build up in the upper regions of abdomen, which was a daily routine, I was falling asleep.

My body felt a deep relaxation. My brain seemed to expand- as if the neurons were swelling up, cell by cell. My eyes were closed, and I was quite aware of myself on bed.

In my mind's eye, I could see a bright light and I was sure it wasn't from outside. My heart was palpitating and as I held it with my palms, I could see a light emanating from my heart. I was rooted, I knew it wasn't a hallucination. And immediately after, I could see a bust level light formation of Lord Venkateshwara of Tirupati. My hands tremble as I write this and I am having goose bumps. It took me a few seconds to register the significance of all that was happening. I lay quietly and I could hear voices within of me, that were not mine, as they were of a different timbre. They were soft and mostly only male voices and it was all happening inside me. There were a few requests from the Lord Himself- request? I was wondering. *He was requesting me!*

The first was that I should not react or say anything to anyone, until time was ripe. Not even to family members.

The second, that the darkest areas of my being would be visited, to pull out and discard, so some discomfort would be experienced. And the methods of grounding and breathing would be taught to me.

The third, I was not to pray or meditate and the shlokas I had to recite or the Bollywood songs I would learn to sing would be presented to me as and when required. Singing is a passion. (The choice of songs that were presented to me, were simply beautiful ones and would love to share the names of these songs one day☺).

The fourth, I had to cull my curiosity. I was not to Google anything without permission. Whatever information I required would be directed towards me, as and when required.

The fifth, I had to pay close attention to my body.

The experiment had begun and I was playing Guinea pig, LOL. There was no fear inside me, just curiosity about how all this could be happening. Two thoughts were comforting to me - that I was in my senses, completely aware of myself and that if this is happening, then its part of nature and anyone can experience it.

A beautiful conversation had begun. I was captivated. The voice of the Lord himself was a soft and gentle one. Sometimes there was subtle humor, and I could say that I was not prepared to believe what was being said. There was also laughter. Each voice of different timbre, crystal clear.

The language of communication was English and sometimes Hindi, I could hear a distinct Uttar Pradesh accent the voice that said "Mind clear hai".

I asked the burning question- why had I not been able to express adequately to my Mom, the deep love I felt for her and how could I say sorry to her?

I was first told that both my parents are safe with Him. I was asked to touch my navel- for I had no navel, just a scar from an operation for umbilical hernia- done at age3, not in my awareness., at the behest of my Dad, for cosmetic reasons.

If scars remind patients of surgeries and success of overcoming a setback, the navel reminds us of our mother, a time to show gratitude, for life. I had lived with the scar and it had not mattered to me that I did not have a navel. The navel is the watershed area for Sympathetic and Vagus nerve, the scar had inactivated corresponding neurons in the brain, the area for showing externally, the love for one's mother. And therefore, though I felt deeply about Mom, I couldn't express it externally.

But the scar had done something good- I had many faults, but anger was never one of them. And I had no worry or fear of future... So, my sympathetic stress was never an issue. This had made me a patient and a better person.

As a reader, it may be difficult to believe that such a conversation is even possible. Since that night, every aspect of my past life (I had not much work to be done on future worries) has been reconstructed to show me how I have made every adversity an opportunity to become what I am.

Who would have thought that a mere scar of umbilical hernia operation (Childhood trauma)- guilt of non-expression of love to mother- food intolerance?

Unless God himself arrives to let me know?

And what better way to of saying thanks than eating all the yummy food that I was once intolerant to!

So now as a Wellness expert, I take down carefully any history of surgery, big or small. For who knows there, may lie the last piece of the puzzle for the patient.

8.2

The Day After and Then Onward

In the wee hours of the morning, which felt between 2.00 -3.00 am, I suddenly felt a sensation of something being fixed inside my brain. So, I sat up, with a start, and then I could see, midway of my brain, light in the formation of the 64 dot figure mentioned in the movie "Thrive" and when I tilted my head, the figure of a lotus. I had read that The Sahasrara Chakra is of Lotus pattern.

I still wasn't sure but I wanted to feel myself on the ground so I walked to the kitchen had a couple of glasses of water. I had a close look at the photo of Divya Dampadi (Lord Venkateshwara and his consort, Padmavati) in the God's room that overlooks the kitchen, nothing amiss. So I walked back to my room and I felt steady. I was good.

Soon I fell asleep.

When my eyes opened, it was around 7.00 am. I may have had about 4 hours of sleep, but I felt new, fresh and extremely happy, a blissfulness that i had never felt before. As I was making my bed, I found the room unusually radiant, considering that the window curtain was only half drawn. There was extreme clarity in my whole being and I was feeling light.

I brushed and A got me the fresh aromatic coffee, like every day. I tried to be normal, bathed and tried my hand at cooking, as if nothing had happened, but found it difficult to focus on the cooking. So I excused myself for rest and requested A to take over, and he complied as he was used to doing this every time I would fall sick with severe GERD. He probably thought I was hyper acidic. The hard bed in our room felt good.

I was feeling some kind of transmission but couldn't actually place it. But this was not troubling me at all. There was no headache nor any pain anywhere, so I wasn't sick either. I hadn't a diagnosis for what I was feeling so just called it "sheer bliss" if that can be a diagnosis.

As if destined to happen, my doctor friend brought us something she had cooked(this was a favorite ritual). Seeing me "down" she enquired what was wrong and I remember telling her that that everything seemed right that I was feeling happy and that I was sensing a transmission of some sort. My friend understandably so must have gotten worried enough to discuss this with my another doctor friend and together they felt that I was allowing my self-experimentations to carry on too far!

I somehow could not bring myself to describe anything to them.

For 4 nights (strangely, every difficult change would happen only in the night, unaware to A and my son). I experienced pain the gall bladder area and wretching but no serious vomiting. Days were generally good and I could carry on with some everyday activities and even manage to go for walks with my son.

Slowly all the awareness that I had received found a way to express in my body. All the thoughts were pulled out of hiding and were flushed down the body, as I introduced one food after another.

In the course of one month, every disease was expressed in my body and as a doctor, I understood disease causation right from its origin.....

Every disease, including epilepsy, which my mother had suffered of. I had a small version of grand mal convulsion but in awareness. I felt how it could be for a person suffering of epilepsy.

Every psychiatric disease from severe depression to psychosis, together with visual hallucinations were expressed.

I understood how past memory can be flushed out and one can start afresh. But what could happen if these were held and how would dementia feel.

I was made to understand what it means to clear out past memory and come to present. All methods of coming to present were shown to me.

It wasn't difficult at all, I must say. Not in the least scary. I was curious and mostly in amazement and wonderment and totally humbled by the gentle methods and gradual ways one small step at a time- Kaizen, they call it in Japanese.

It was beautiful and humbling, and my being was filled with Gratitude for the benevolence being showered on me.

I was made aware of who I was, why I have A as my dear husband and purpose of my lovely children. I was made aware how the girls from my school were links from the past.

The entire spectrum of me as "I" and my relation with every component of the environment was explained. That even as biological creatures, we all follow laws of quantum physics. E= mC2. It was as if life had come a full circle.

My family was happy because I was now eating everything and was happy, so they never spooked and I had all I needed for the transformation- water, food and plenty of oxygen out of the canopy and most of all a caring family. It felt exhilarating.

About 10 days after NOH, I was beginning to feel slightly dense, in mind and body and I knew that very soon I was going to feel fully grounded, just like before.

8.3

The Ultimate Humbling Moment

Nature is our best teacher and we just need to hold the trust

I was feeling young again, approximately 25, but to others I would say, about 40 years. My GERD had reduced by 90%, my IBS was a thing of past. I was feeling vibrant and I was feeling love, for everything that was Life. "Life is beautiful" had been my WhatsApp status ever since I had started using the app. And I was sleeping well.

A month after NOH, I was urged to be seated in a comfortable reclining chair (which I now call "Vikramaditya's throne" LOL) in my living room. On sitting there, I could distinctly hear a high frequency sound against the silence of the dark night- this was the first time I heard it, the frequency of transmission.

As I closed my eyes, as per instructions (remember I was not to meditate until asked), I could see nothing but a blank diffuse light in the fore head area (which approximately corresponds to the frontal lobe of the brain which is the area of stored memory). Previously I would see the Lord's figure or I would be able to invoke it- in Ophthalmological terms this is called "Persistence of Vision"

That night, I was not able to- I had met the "Ultimate Source", the Original Source, the Nothingness. I had met myself the way I was born!!

I felt totally humbled, to the core of my being and I sat there and cried and cried. I spent an hour and went back to the room and soon fell asleep. I slept like a baby; pun intended.

The next morning, I realized how really simple it is to become one with nature and if Life appears complicated, it is mostly our doing.

When all the stress is removed and there is no more stress to be removed, and one hears the high frequency of transmission, one is very close to the Bat in nature but sophisticated in the built- and the corona virus can just remain in the nasal tracts without really affecting you. And of course, one would wear a mask until everyone around is helped to simplify to level of the Bat. And one is not day blind, so the East can be figured out!!!!

And when one's body can be a home to corona viruses to such a degree of acceptance and trust in oneself to rise to the calling, its only easy to figure out that energy forms of our guiding spirits, from whichever corner of the world, from America to India or any place on Earth, can enter and leave, like one would do in one's home! Because they are now secure in their home.

As I sat watching a documentary on the making of Bond 007 movies, I heard Barbara Broccoli say that her father, Albert Broccoli, the celebrated maker of Bond movies, resides inside of her and that's where she derives her strength from, I can relate to it completely.

I can hear my Mom and Dad from inside of me, guiding my actions. I know I am sorted, for life!!

And the feeling is sublime.

8.4

The Final Chapter- What's that?

For a being of total trust, Life is a continuum- between the physical and metaphysical, between the seen and the unseen.

Life is beautiful when it is explored with curiosity and self- honesty.

As a doctor colleague of mine said, most "physical" phenomena of electricity and gravity are unseen and we can only feel their effects. Just because one cannot provide proof of physicality, does not mean it does not exist.

When there is trust, there is no fear and one can "just be" in the moment.

And when one can "just be" as part of Nature and Universe, one would definitely want to allow every other being to "just be" too. And suddenly there's love, compassion, co-operation and selflessness- the heady mix of life itself- the very things you are born for and to experience. When this mix is iced with the sugar of curiosity, we reap the complete benefit of being born as Homo sapiens sapiens☺

Every human being has access to this miracle- since the requirements are nothing more than water, food, oxygen and an understanding family such as mine. And TRUST.

As tears of joy flow, I say that Life is worth every moment. It is for us to see its beauty and potential.